A

Our mission is to provide readers with a pocket-sized read in the places where they are waiting, relaxing, taking a break. We aim to support writers by giving them a new market for their short stories and short non-fiction.

Don't forget to visit our website www.leafbooks.co.uk to tell us what you think of this book and to learn more about the writer and our other services.

Enjoy!

First published by Leaf Books Ltd in 2006
Copyright © William D. Gill

Cover illustration © Gavin Pugh

Leaf Books are proud to be working with
The University of Glamorgan

www.leafbooks.co.uk

Leaf
GTi Suite,
Valleys Innovation Centre,
Navigation Park,
Abercynon,
CF45 4SN

Printed by Allprint
www.allprint.ltd.uk

ISBN 1-905599-13-7
ISBN 978-1-905599-13-4

Confidence

by

William D. Gill

leaf
14

William D. Gill once loved a girl so much he joined the army to be with her. Seventeen years later, they are still married and have five children. A native of Mississippi, he earned degrees in history and pharmacy from The University of Kentucky and now practices pharmacy in his adopted hometown of Lexington, Kentucky. Most recently his essay, 'Imitating Art: Guy Cobb, Shelby Farms, and the Distillation of Life and Place,' was anthologized in *Story South: The Best of the South 2005*. He is currently at work on *The Noxubee Refuge*, a novel about the not so rural South.

Confidence

I have a premonition that I will be killed in a convenience store hold-up or die in some similar ignominious way. I'll be shot shortly after some idiot with a gun starts flashing it at the cashier, punctuating the air with obscenities and threats, demanding the paltry assortment of paper money in the cash drawer. Maybe I'll be shot for trying to bring calm to the situation. Maybe I'll be speaking in soothing terms, having just said, 'Look, let's all stay cool, and everybody'll be okay,' ready to issue forth more wisdom when the bullet hits me in the forehead. Maybe, more likely, I will be petrified, won't say anything, will get plugged nonetheless and bleed out quickly on the dirty tile floor, still clutching the Snickers bar that was inadvertently the cause of my death. Either way, it will be over for me. Endgame. All very fast and for no good reason. Or maybe I'll get run over by the Meals on Wheels van, or die on the toilet like Elvis. I'm sure it will happen in the most disconcerting way. No glory, just death: a death everyone would prefer to forget. A death that I would prefer everyone forget.

When I was eleven, my summer city-league baseball team was the Bluejays. We were a decent team with perhaps the best pitcher in the league, John Luzner. He was the best until he got hit in the temple by a line drive off one of his fastballs. I saw the whole play clearly from the vantage point of third base.

I was covering for the regular third baseman at the time, Nick Fleenor. Nick had a reoccurring problem with his spastic colon and was sitting this game out. That Nick had a spastic colon was bad enough, but what was immeasurably worse for Nick was his mother's need to attend every game and make sure that everyone else knew that her 'little Nicky' had a spastic colon. It was a serious medical condition she assured, and if anyone pretended to be unfamiliar with it, she did her best to educate said person in whatever time was available, sparing no detail about the bloating, the diarrhea, the cramping and the 'frequent accidents' that made a normal life for her child impossible.

In the accentuated slow motion of my memory I see it happen in a perfect replay and have seen it such a thousand times at least. I will see it ever more clearly time and again until I pass from this world, a richness of detail and color that gets a little cleaner and brighter and more precise with each viewing, like a classic film that is being endlessly enhanced and digitally remastered, until the end result is completely adulterated. The blue of the uniforms is too vibrant. Sunlight breaks through the cloud bank and the whole scene looks like a living Bierstadt painting. The grass glows like a field of crushed emerald.

From third, I see John's windup, his textbook delivery and the bead of a fastball heading for the plate. The batter is a big boy, probably a good 150 pounds of fat and muscle. He cranks his bat into the pitch and rifles the leather back to the mound.

John doesn't duck. He crouches half a foot, turns his head to the side, and throws up his glove to protect his face. His glove is too high, resting more on top of his head than in front. The ball comes in below the thumb and strikes him in the temple.

For every time I see the ball hit him, I see him drop three times. He just keeps dropping, collapsing to the ground like a vanquished middle-weight who has taken an uppercut to his glass jaw. I stand immobile. Coaches and players are trotting to the mound. The crowd is quiet except for a woman who is screaming, calling out John's name as if it has the power to make him rise. I can see her in the bleachers. People are attempting to restrain her. She is John's mother, or grandmother, or aunt, or maybe she doesn't even know John at all. Perhaps, like so many other people, she just feels the need to wail. Her voice sounds faint out at third, like it's being broadcast through the speaker of a cheap portable radio.

I look back to the mound. There are three players standing close, staring down on two kneeling adults who are examining John. They have turned him on his back, and he lies unresponsive to their mild shakes and finger snapping. He has only fallen a distance less than his height, but he may as well have fallen out of the sky from a passing airplane.

I see him fall again. His head stops the ball and for an instant it stops moving as it transfers its kinetic force to the boy's temple. When the transfer is complete, John falls and the ball careens off to the side and after a couple of bounces, rolls to a stop between second and third. The shortstop is not there to notice. He has run up to the pitcher's mound, but he slows as he gets close, content to stare at the adults who have already assumed prominence above the victim.

I didn't move. I watched the shortstop, the first baseman and the catcher converge in the middle of the diamond, but I stood behind the baseline as surely as if it had been the boundary of a crime scene. I was certain of the outcome and there was no point in fighting for what was already lost. That was, I believe, the first time I publicly displayed my lack of hope.

I mouthed a prayer with the team, as we all

stood in a huddle around the coach, while the ambulance pulled out of the park on its way to Central Baptist. The whooping of the siren bled over the closing. Most of the boys had tear streaks, dark brown canals through the dust on their faces and they walked off confusedly into the arms of their moms and dads. My mother was there, looking grim and waiting behind the backstop. She wanted to comfort me, but I wasn't crying.

In my mind I kept seeing John drop. One second he was standing, the next he was on the ground. Normally, I wouldn't have been on third to see it. Now, I would see it forever. When John died two days later, I did cry, but I didn't know why, because for me it had all been over the moment he fell. The finality was in the collapse, but I didn't cry that day. I only cried at the institutional confirmation of my own private certainty. I cried at the proof of a horrible truth, at the illumination of the fragile web on which we climb.

*

'Why are you so fascinated with death?' asks Callie. She is my girl, Callie, her name short for Calliope, and she is as musical and poetic as her namesake. She is my polar opposite, being blonde and fair and blue-eyed. She is as light on her feet as an elf and sometimes I halfway expect to glimpse a pointed auricle when the wind blows back the sides of her uncomplicated hair.

Callie is most always happy, what others would call 'bubbly', and does not understand my malaise. She thinks, I believe, that I am afflicted in some ancient way. Perhaps that I am burdened with a demon. This is easy for her to believe in light of her other beliefs, for she believes in God the father, Jesus, the Holy Spirit, the communion of saints, the devil, a hierarchy of angelic and demonic beings, spiritual warfare, eternal judgment, Heaven, Hell, world without end, etcetera. She is convinced that my malaise is spiritual in nature and in that she may very well be right. She is as uncomplicated as her hair.

We are sitting in a meadow at the

cemetery. Two hundred years of headstones and monuments adorn the undulating hills of bluegrass. The angels surrounding us convey hopefulness in their posture and their presence, but it is a hope wrapped in sadness, a hope both solid and cold like the marble and limestone from which they are carved. They are beautiful with aquiline faces and shoulder length hair, neuter in form and framed by the wings on their backs. They stand tall to watch over the dead and the many living who will soon be dead.

A demijohn of red wine pokes up from under the lid of our wicker picnic basket. We have come to rest beneath a poplar tree, to inhale the essence of an autumn day, two young mortals in the glow of health. We are as full and ripe as a pair of unblemished peaches, no sign of decay upon our skin, and we sit among the gravestones digesting the experience of life. My five senses are tingling; my stomach is full. A cool breeze kisses my neck and I feel a knot of love moving around like a butterfly in my thoracic region. I am on the verge of contentment, and I imagine that if I could only get there then joy would be right over the horizon.

Callie is smiling. The sun sparkles in her hair. She can look out over the landscape of burned out wicks and melted candle wax and not find sadness in the finality or the futility of it all. Like the candle, we are made for a purpose and once that purpose is achieved, our wax is gone and our wick goes out, she would say. Maybe this explains why she lights candles and I can't bear to. The candles in my apartment are few and all remain as they were when the candle maker dipped them. I deny them their fate much as I long for someone or something to deny me mine. One more finished candle, placed in a wooden box, packed in earth, my dust held in place by the rock of a marker that rests heavy on top like a paperweight: this is not my desire.

'I'm not fascinated with death,' I say. This, as far as I can introspectively discern, is the truth. Death is only symptomatic of a larger problem.

*

Another day. The cemetery is relegated to memory and that seems so strange, for much gets misplaced when experience goes into memory. Gone is the sensory data and all that remains is a visual template, packed away to fade like a photograph left in sunlight. I remember the knot in my stomach, but as a memory it is in my mind and not in my stomach any more.

Fall is more dominant today. There is a snap in the air and the wind is gusting. The flags downtown were popping taut as I walked to my aunt's house, the lanyards banging against the hollow metal of the poles. It was the mournful sound of a muffled bell and it blended with the angry whistle of the wind in such a way to cause me discomfort.

But I am warm now. Inside and seated in a plush chair, I have a Burmese cat at my feet. Above, the fat chandelier burns low. My aunt sits to my side on the couch. She is a gray haired woman, dainty and proud, apt to talk and not to listen, though possessed of enough sense to usually be close to the mark in her personal observations. She pours me a cup of Oolong tea from her delicate Limoge pot. The porcelain is so thin as to be translucent, and I can see the meniscus of tea through the pattern of violets that graces the cup. Everything seems perfect. A plate of brittle cookies sits between our cups. I lean close to the table and the steam grants me a perception of the subtle complexity yet to meet my tongue. I am almost afraid to move.

With the exception of the chair that holds me, all of the furniture in this room, she says, is from the nineteenth century or prior. This does not put me at ease, though I am sure I knew it already. This knowledge is, in fact, the reason why I have chosen the chair. It is more modern and more solid and I feel more certain of its ability to withstand my presence. I have been here before, though I can't remember the specific instance of when. I have a memory, but it is vague. Rather, it is a series of similar memories, all indistinguishable and out of sequence, combined in my head to form a summary. I have a knowledge of this room and it is always the same. And my aunt, she is always the same. The two are symbiotic, the room and my aunt. I never see one without the other and neither seems to ever change. Hence, I can't remember the last time I was here.

'What have you decided to do with your life?' she asks. She is the sister of my father's first wife and the only relative who remains with me in Kentucky. Married young and into money, she survived the early death of her husband and has lived in an immaculate three storey Victorian house across from Transylvania University since before my birth. From behind the many windows of her home, she is a keen observer of the human condition, though for her life is more of a book than a journey. She has no scars as far as I can tell, save for the early death of her husband, but that must have healed nicely because she never mentions him. She is not afraid to display fragile items.

I stare into the blackness of my Oolong. I

should at least be comforted by it. It seems so certain, so therapeutic, so removed from the day to day struggle. The ground–up leaves of tea once buoyed an empire. But the empire crumbled. Though the tea is still consumed, it is vestigial, a reminder of what once was. Nor is it very therapeutic. Too much tea means too much theophylline and my heart will race. It is, upon analysis, a bitter drink. Stripped of its warmth it is not much better than the wind I have left outside.

My aunt puts sugar in her tea to hide the bitterness. She seeks to control her life like she controls her tea, but I think she asks the wrong question of me. Sturdy walls that have sheltered others shelter her from the bitter wind, but outside the wind still blows and inside the clock still ticks. 'What has life decided to do with me?' I ask her in return.

She makes a face between sips and speaks of free will. I sit quietly and listen. I don't know what to make of free will. There is either acceptance or denial. Is that the same as free will?

*

'You need to make some friends,' says my mother. She speaks from the phone in my hand. Far away in Florida she is reclining at the poolside. 'Come down to Ft. Lauderdale. There are plenty of nice people your age down here. You'll be able to make some wonderful friends.' My mother speaks of friendship in terms of geography or income. She claims there is more affluence and style in Ft. Lauderdale than in the whole state of Kentucky.

'I have Callie,' I say.

'Yes,' she says, and her voice trails off. She is not speaking of girlfriends, my mother. She thinks I am too consumed by the world of women. She blames herself for the divorce, for the loss of a male role-model in my life. Try as she might, she could not be a father to me and the limitations of this fact haunt her in my presence. There is probably truth in her concern. I know this but can do nothing about it. If it were possible to interview all the young men in Lexington, then I would be sure to find a friend. Short of that I am left with the guys I knew at the university and the guys with whom I work. They are nice enough guys, most of them. I know their language. I can shoot the bull with the best of them. We talk of fishing and UK sports, politics and cigars. I can stand tall beside them. I get invited to gatherings at bars and restaurants. In April and October, I am frequently asked to attend the races at Keeneland. 'You should place a few bets,' I am told. 'We'll have a blast.'

I seldom go anymore. I act as if I will, but inevitably I call to say that something came up. I'm sorry. Maybe next time. They are too self-assured, the guys I know. They all seem to have a plan, some path they are carving with a definite endpoint in mind. They are like Alexander on his way to the Indus.

'You always seem to be around girls and women,' says my mother. She is being blunt with me now. She must really be worried, for it is too early in the day for her to be drinking.

'I like girls,' I reply.

'So did your father.' It is a throw-away line,

better left unsaid. I cringe for her. 'I'm glad you like girls, honey.' She is trying to regroup. 'I didn't mean to imply…'

'Besides, Callie isn't just any girl.'

There is a prolonged hesitation on the line. She is weighing my statement and trying to flesh out the implications. 'I'm sure Callie is very special. Just don't get tied down.' My mother is concerned about my freedom. Yet she wants me to come down to Ft. Lauderdale where she can keep an eye on me. Freedom from what?

*

'You appear to be perfectly fit.' My doctor is sitting to my right, making notes in my chart. I am buttoning my shirt. 'How do you feel?' she asks.

'Okay,' I answer.

'You'll live to be a hundred,' she smiles.

'You're sure?'

'Well, anything could happen.' She studies my face. 'I don't get many people requesting complete physicals in their early twenties.'

'I'm just trying to gather as much information as possible,' I say.

'About what?'

'Myself,' I say.

She crosses her legs. 'Are you worried about something?'

I shift uneasily and the paper on the examination table crinkles a bit too loud. I feel odd sitting higher than my physician, looking down on her as she looks up at me. 'I saw a boy get killed with a baseball once.'

'When was this?' she asks. Her eyes are larger than they were. A simple wedding band encircles her left ring finger and it occurs to me why I am more comfortable around women. They can never get too settled with their lives. The knowledge of impending motherhood can rupture their plans like an icebreaker.

'A long time ago,' I say.

'Do you need to talk with someone about it? I can write you a consult.'

'I'm already getting help.'

'From a psychiatrist?'

'From a friend.'

'I see.' She stands and puts a hand on the door knob. 'I can start you on an anti-depressant if you would like.'

'I'm not depressed.'

'They're not only for depression. They can help with anxiety too. A low dose of Paxil might help.'

'I'm not anxious.'

'It's not habit forming.'

'I'm okay.' If I have to worry about something being habit forming, then how can it be beneficial? Whatever happened to the concept of good habits?

'Call my office if I can help. Oh, I'll have the results of you urine and blood work by Friday.'

'Thanks.'

Callie is waiting in the lobby, reading *O* magazine. 'You don't need Oprah to tell you how to live,' I say.

She takes my hand. 'So how are you?'

Outside, as we make our way to my car, I look out over the leafless trees that dot the parking lot. 'It's winter soon,' I say.

'The sky is still blue,' says Callie.

'There's nothing wrong with my body.'

'I could have told you that.'

'I mean on the inside.'

'That too.'

I stare at Callie after unlocking her door. She stands for a few seconds smiling, her hair captured in the wind and her eyes bluer than the sky that frames her head. She is beautiful to me in a way that defies category. To think that I can't live without her presumes that I can live at all. I am frightened at the limb on which I find my thoughts, but at the end of that limb is Callie. She is a fruit that dangles from the tree of life.

'What?' she asks.

'What do you mean?'

'You've a strange look on your face.'

Embarrassed, I avert my gaze down to the car, to the sheet of white paint that covers the roof. As automobiles go, it is functional and sturdy, if not exactly stylish. It has served me well for more than three years, but suddenly I don't want to climb inside. I have no desire to crank the engine and join the river of traffic that flows in front of the medical complex. It seems insane to strap oneself inside a combination of glass, steel and combustible fuel. I shake my head to break my train of thought and look back up at Callie. 'You have something I want,' I say bluntly.

'I know,' she says with a sly smile.

'Not that!'

'Really?' she says. Concern fills her eyes.

'Not just that,' I clarify.

'What then?' she asks, smiling again.

'How do you know the sky won't fall any second?'

'I don't.'

'And?'

'And I'd rather have a full stomach if it does. I'd also rather be inside the car,' she hints.

I oblige and open her door, making my pensive way to the driver's side. Callie laughs and talks of Indian food as we pull from the parking lot. Soon the air is permeated with the smell of her perfume: spices, citrus and vanilla, all intermingled with the unique ineffable fragrance of Callie. It is the smell of all I desire, of all I cannot deny and long to accept. Of that, at least, I am confident.

**Runner-up in the
Leaf Short Story
Competition**

**DOPPELGANGER
Simon Todd**

'It was him, his double, his twin, his exact other, then mysteriously the other smiled and was gone.'

It is said that somewhere in the world, we all have our shadow walkers, our exact doubles and seeing them forecasts our own imminent death.

**Runner-up in the
Leaf Short Story
Competition**

**THE GIFT
Ghislaine Goff**

'I had given him a gift that had sparked a war; now it was time to give him one which would end it.'

Guillaume de Rais, Principal Herald of France, is proud of his professional detachment. In medieval Europe, heralds are diplomats, the guardians of chivalry and umpires of battle – they ensure that the rules are kept. But when detachment becomes impossible, Guillaume discovers that he can no longer keep the rules.

WAITING A WHILE FOR GREENEYES
Marian Van Eyk McCain

'A certain woman's name flashing up on my screen ...'

At first, she's just another member of an Internet forum on 21st Century physics. He knows her only by her nickname: Greeneyes. But when he volunteers to take part in her mysterious experiment, Dan's life suddenly takes a strange new turn.

For more information about Leaf Books and our services, please visit our website:

www.leafbooks.co.uk

- Complete List of Leaf Books
- Writers' Biographies
- Readers' Forum
- Ebooks
- Audio Books
- MP3 Downloadable Books
- Stockists
- How to Submit a Story to Leaf
- Competitions
- Writers' Services
- Jobs with Leaf

Competitions and Submissions

The Leaf competition and submission calendar enables us to gather stories, non-fiction, poetry written by new and established writers in the UK and abroad.

Every entry or submission is read by at least two members of our readers' panel. The panel consists of book and story lovers who represent a wide selection of backgrounds and tastes. We are very proud of this selection procedure and believe it gives a fair chance to every writer who sends us their work.

Leaf Competitions Entry Form

Name_____
Address_____
_____
_____
Email _____
Phone_____
Competition Title _____
See www.leafbooks.co.uk for details of
Competitions and closing dates.
Title of Story/Piece/Poem
1._____
2._____
3._____
4._____
I enclose cheque, made payable to Leaf, for
£_____ (£5.00 for each story, £2.50 for
each poem, and £10 for each critique).
Please send entries to:
Leaf, Gti Suite, Valleys Innovation Centre
Abercynon, CF45 4SN.